Princess Poppy
A True Princess

*Check out Princess Poppy's website
to find out all about the other
books in the series*

www.princesspoppy.com

Princess Poppy
A True Princess

written by Janey Louise Jones
Illustrated by Samantha Chaffey

A TRUE PRINCESS
A YOUNG CORGI BOOK 978 0 552 55594 4

First published in Great Britain by Young Corgi,
an imprint of Random House Children's Books

Young Corgi edition published 2007

5 7 9 10 8 6 4

Papers used by Random House Children's Books are natural, recyclable
products made from wood grown in sustainable forests. The manufacturing
processes conform to the environmental regulations of the country of origin.

The Random House Group Limited makes every effort to ensure that the
papers used in its books are made from trees that have been legally sourced
from well-managed and credibly certified forests. Our paper procurement
policy can be found at: www.randomhouse.co.uk/paper.htm

Mixed Sources
Product group from well-managed
forests and other controlled sources
www.fsc.org Cert no. TF-COC-2139
© 1996 Forest Stewardship Council
FSC

Set in 14/21pt Bembo MT Schoolbook by
Falcon Oast Graphic Art Ltd.

Young Corgi Books are published by Random House Children's Books,
61–63 Uxbridge Road, London W5 5SA,
a division of The Random House Group Ltd

Addresses for companies within The Random House Group Limited can be
found at: www.randomhouse.co.uk/offices.htm

THE RANDOM HOUSE GROUP Limited Reg. No. 954009
www.kidsatrandomhouse.co.uk
www.princesspoppy.com

A CIP catalogue record for this book is available from the British Library.

Printed in the UK by CPI William Clowes Ltd,
Beccles, NR34 7TL

With thanks to Alice Corrie
for her dedication to Princess Poppy

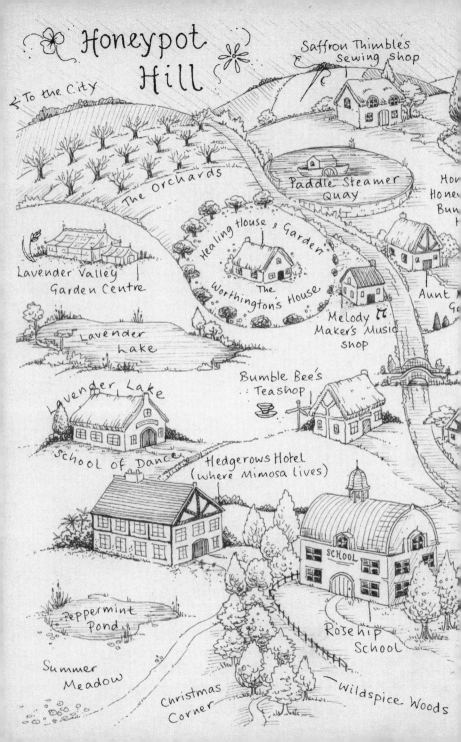

Chapter One

Poppy often thought about what she might be when she grew up. Usually she imagined that she was a princess living in a pale sandstone palace, wearing a beautiful dress complete with a diamond tiara. It was one of Poppy's dreams to visit a real palace one day, where a real princess had actually lived.

Her best friend Honey had been taken to a palace in the city once, when her mum and dad came to visit. Poppy was still very jealous of that. In fact, even though Honey

1

hardly ever saw her parents, Poppy was always envious of her friend when they did visit because they did wonderful things with Honey and took her to amazing places. Honey's parents were away working most of the time so she was looked after by her grandmother, Granny Bumble. But when her mum and dad did see Honey, they really spoiled her. What Poppy didn't realize was that Honey would much rather have seen them every day than be given big treats once in a while. She missed her mum and dad so much when they were working.

"I've hardly seen Honey recently, now that her parents are here," Poppy complained to no one in particular. "Every day she seems to go on a fancy trip and I'm stuck here with Mum and her big baby tummy for company!"

This was the complete opposite of what normally happened. Honey practically lived

with Poppy most of the time. The two girls were inseparable and Honey really looked up to her best friend. Poppy adored Honey too: even though they'd once had a huge falling out over the ballet show, they'd made up in the end – they always did.

Poppy loved ballet. In certain moods she dreamed of becoming a ballerina when she grew up rather then a princess. In her mind she could imagine curtseying on the stage at Covent Garden after performing *Swan Lake*, just like Madame Angelwing had many years ago. But the truth was that Honey was a better dancer and Poppy was starting to think she might not be good enough to be a famous ballerina after all.

At other times Poppy thought she would like to be a schoolteacher. She loved Miss Mallow, her teacher at Rosehip School. As well as being a brilliant teacher, Miss Mallow made fabulous jewellery. But Poppy often thought that Honey was Miss Mallow's favourite: whenever there were new pupils at school, Honey was *always* asked to show them around. Poppy thought this was very unfair – she would have loved to do that job and she was sure she would be really good at it too!

Today Poppy didn't dream of being a princess or a ballerina or even a teacher. She dreamed of being a nurse. She didn't know anyone who actually was a nurse, but she knew that she loved looking after other people and animals, especially her hamster Posy and her pony Twinkletoes. She also took very good care of her many soft toys and dolls, particularly when she thought they weren't feeling well. Poppy really enjoyed making others feel better so she thought she might be a rather good nurse. Perhaps the fact that Aunt Marigold, Mimosa and Madame Angelwing had all come down with a horrible bout of flu had given her the nurse idea – Poppy wasn't sure, but she hoped they would all feel better soon and that no one else in the village would come down with it. It also occurred to her that when Mum had the babies, she would have to learn to look after them too, especially if they were ever sick. Grandpa had told her that they would be quite a handful — whatever that meant!

"I had better start practising to be a good nurse," Poppy said to Ruby, her big rag doll.

She sat on her bedroom floor and opened the hospital kit that Grandpa had given her last Christmas. But before she started on her nursing jobs she began to think about what had happened to her the day before, and as she did so, a hard lump came into her throat and she felt as if she might cry. It was all so unfair . . .

Chapter Two

Saffron had phoned Mum to see if Poppy
would like to model some children's fashion
accessories and clothes over at her shop. The local
newspaper, the Honeypot Herald, was doing
a feature on the shop and was sending a
photographer over.

"How exciting – I'm going to be a model. I'm
going to be famous – of course I would like to!"
Poppy cried when Mum told her about it. "But I
will have to wash my hair first, it's really dirty."

"Oh, Poppy! Your hair will take ages to dry and

you might miss the photographer – he's far too busy to hang around all day," said Mum. "Why don't I just brush it for you?"

"Mum! If I'm going to be in a newspaper, I want to have clean shiny hair," said Poppy stubbornly as she raced up to the bathroom.

Mum was right. Poppy's hair did take a long time to dry even with the hairdryer.

When Poppy and Mum finally arrived at Saffron's shop Honey was already being photographed. She was dressed in a fabulous purple skirt with a pink top, gorgeous lilac glass beads and a sequinned hairband. She looked great!

"That should be enough pictures now, Saffron," said the photographer. "What a great kid Honey is. She's stunning, and a natural in front of the camera!"

Poppy couldn't believe it. She had only arrived a tiny bit later than Honey but she had completely missed her chance to be photographed.

She was very angry and upset – mainly with

herself for taking so long with her hair – so she stomped off in a grump.

"Poppy, don't go off in a bad mood," said Saffron. "I'm really sorry. The photographer was in a rush and Honey got here first and it was all very last minute. I'm sure you'll have another chance to get in the local paper."

But Poppy was feeling quite tearful and did not reply. It seemed to her as if Honey was always getting to do all the things she wanted to do – life was so unfair!

As Poppy headed for the door, she caught the sleeve of her crocheted cardigan on Saffron's jewellery stand and accidentally pulled the whole thing over. All the gorgeous sparkly necklaces, earrings, bracelets and rings crashed to the floor.

Poppy turned round to look at the mess. "I'm really sorry, Saffron . . . I didn't mean to . . ." she began between sobs. "I'll clear it up for you."

Saffron looked furious. "Poppy! I hope you didn't do that on purpose," she said sharply.

"No, I didn't. Honestly. I promise. I would never do something like that deliberately," said Poppy.

But Saffron's face showed that she didn't know whether to believe Poppy or not.

As Poppy began to pick up the jewellery that was lying on the floor and put it back onto the stand, Honey came back from the dressing room.

"Well done, Honey, and thanks so much for

coming at such short notice. I can't wait to see the photos in the newspaper. Here's a little something for you," Saffron said as she handed Honey the beads she had modelled.

"Wow, thanks! It was great fun, though it would have been even better to do it with Poppy," smiled Honey. "I'm going to the city to do some shoe shopping with my dad now. Yippee!"

Poppy shuddered as she remembered how she had felt when she left the shop with Saffron's frosty "Goodbye, Poppy," ringing in her ears. She loved Saffron and really looked up to her. It was very important to Poppy that Saffron thought highly of her, so the fact that she didn't believe her about the jewellery stand upset her terribly. Poor Poppy wasn't even sure if Mum believed that it was an accident either. Poppy felt as if nobody liked or trusted her any more.

But she tried to put all that out of her

mind. Poppy had decided to practise
her nursing skills by turning her
bedroom into a Healing Herb
Hospital. She was sure that would
make her feel better. She brought in
a bundle of herbs from the garden:
mint, rosemary and lots of lavender,
because Grandpa said that lavender
helped to soothe problems and he
knew almost everything about
plants. Poppy was sure Grandpa
was right because if she ever felt
troubled, she would go to the
Lavender Garden and the amazing
smell of the lavender plants always
calmed her down and made her
problems melt away. Last year,
when Poppy was in the Lavender
Garden mulling over a problem, she
had sketched each of the herbs and
flowers she saw and smelled there.

When she got home, with a bit of help from Mum and a big book all about healing herbs, she had made a poster about the herbs and what they could do to make you feel better. The poster was now stuck up on her bedroom wall.

Poppy's Healing Herb Poster

peppermint for colds

sage for fevers!

parsley for spots + rashes

lavender to soothe + relax

rosemary for aches + pains

Poppy looked at her poster now and decided that this time she would make a special medicine out of lavender – it would help her and her patients to feel better.

"It will be a special healing fairy dust made with ground lavender petals," she said to herself.

When she had made the fairy dust, Poppy started getting the rest of the hospital together. She looked all over the house for things to use as makeshift hospital beds – prams, buggies, cushions, even cardboard boxes and her own bed, which would fit quite a few sick toys in! Then she rummaged around in her hospital kit for a nurse's uniform, bandages, plasters, medicines and syringes, and finally she found a pretty little box to put her special healing fairy dust in. Now everything was ready – the Healing Herb Hospital was open for business.

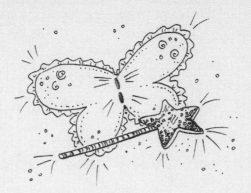

Chapter Three

"Ruby, you have a fever," she said to her big rag doll as she tucked her under a fluffy blanket in the big dolls' pram and gave her some sage leaves to sniff. Ruby looked much more comfortable – that is, until Poppy approached her with a pretend syringe! "Just a little jab, Ruby! It won't hurt a bit," said Poppy, remembering her pre-school jabs and how quickly it had all happened.

She busied herself in her new hospital and was very pleased with how it was going. She felt wanted, useful, organized and kind – a very caring princess. And the toys seemed to like her so much more than everyone else did. Just as she was attending to a teddy with a broken wrist, the doorbell rang and Poppy heard Mum ask someone in. It was Honey!

"Come up and play, Honey!" Poppy called down the stairs.

"Hi, Poppy!" said Honey. "I'm sorry I got to be in the photos yesterday and you didn't. I hope you don't mind too much – I know Saffron wanted to have both of us but the photographer was in a real hurry."

"Oh, it doesn't matter. It's not your fault. It was actually all my own fault because I washed my hair and it took too long to dry. I'm just upset that Saffron could even think that I would tip up that jewellery stand on purpose."

Honey nodded. "I know it was just an accident. You would never do something like that – even if you were in one of your bad tempers!"

"Thanks, Honey," smiled Poppy. "I knew *you* would believe me."

It was nice to see Honey again – somebody did like her after all! And it wasn't Honey's fault about the photographs or all the brilliant trips she was going on. Poppy felt a little of her old confidence coming back.

"What shall we do?" asked Honey.

"I'm playing hospitals," said Poppy. "Join in, it's fun. I'll tell you all about it."

Just as Poppy was about to start explaining, she noticed that Honey was wearing fairy wings, as she often did, but more importantly that she also had a brand-new lavender fairy wand with her.

19

This gave Poppy a really good idea!

"This is my Healing Herb Hospital – I am trying to make all the sick toys better. I am Healing Princess Poppy and I'm in charge of everything. You can be Healing Fairy Honey because you've got a magic wand. You can use it to make the toys well again. Just sprinkle some fairy dust on the end of the wand, then wave it over the patients. I will also need you to take temperatures and give out medicine," explained Poppy, nearly back to her bossy ways again.

"What's fairy dust?" asked Honey.

Poppy explained to Honey what fairy dust was and told her all about the soothing powers of lavender. Then she took her on her hospital round.

"Ruby has a really high fever. Arthur the wooden soldier has a bad leg wound from a fierce battle with Captain Sea-lord. Fenella the tooth fairy puppet has a tummy ache

from eating too many sweets. She takes them away from children when she delivers their silver pennies. And Belinda the pink bunny has terrible earache," continued Poppy, stroking a long white velvet ear on the pretty pink rabbit.

"Poppy!" squealed Honey, interrupting Poppy's flow. "There's something moving in this little blue pram!"

"Yes, I know," replied Poppy calmly. "That is Posy, my little hamster. She's been in a fight and needs a lot of care and attention."

Poppy brushed Posy's white fur with a soft brush and gave her some water from a tiny

21

bottle. When Poppy had finished explaining to Honey what was wrong with all the patients, she settled down to design a chart so that she and Honey could make notes on each of the sick toys – just like real nurses. She drew a picture of each toy, and Posy, and marked in a red arrow pointing to where they were hurting.

"Honey, each time you check on one of our patients, you must draw either a smiley face or a sad face opposite each patient, depending on how they are feeling," said Poppy.

Honey nodded enthusiastically. Poppy liked the way that she was the one who had good ideas and thought up new games, while Honey just enjoyed acting them out and playing along. They were a good team.

The Healing Herb Hospital was looking very clean and tidy and the patients were all resting comfortably after a wave from

Honey's lavender fairy wand. Then Poppy
started trying to bandage Arthur's leg; she
became very impatient when the bandage
got all tangled up, so Honey offered to take
over. Honey made a beautifully neat job
of it. She was so good at things like that.
Poppy complimented her friend but inside
she was annoyed that Honey was better at
bandaging than she was. Poor Poppy was

beginning to feel again that Honey was good at *everything*.

"I think we need a break," said Poppy. "I'll go down and see what there is in the fridge. You keep an eye on the patients."

Poppy's mum was in the sitting room with Cousin Saffron and Poppy could hear the hum of their chat as she walked down the stairs but not what they were actually saying. *Probably moaning about me "tipping the jewellery stand over" yesterday!* she thought gloomily. But as she made her way along the hallway to the kitchen, she could hear them much better and her ears pricked up as soon as she heard her name mentioned . . .

Chapter Four

"Did you have a best friend in the village when you were growing up, Aunt Lavender?" asked Saffron.

"Not really. Of course, I had my family around me but I always longed for a best friend."

"Me too," agreed Saffron. "Poppy is so lucky to have Honey."

"Yes, I know. Honey's a little sweetie, isn't she? So caring and gentle," said Mum.

"That's right," agreed Saffron. "And she's

so pretty, with her wonderful dark hair and brown skin. The photographer thought she was a natural in front of the camera."

Poppy stopped in her tracks. She felt confused and sad to hear Mum and Saffron admiring Honey so much when she herself was in trouble for something she didn't even do.

Everyone thinks Honey is so wonderful, but what about me?

Poppy looked at herself in the mirror in the hallway. Her blonde hair and dark blue eyes were nothing like Honey's gorgeous dark hair and rich chocolate-brown eyes. Sometimes having a perfect best friend was *really* annoying. Poppy carried on to the kitchen, and couldn't hear Mum and Saffron any more, although they were still chatting away merrily, completely unaware that Poppy was even downstairs.

"Of course, Honey is just as lucky to have Poppy as a friend," continued Saffron.

"I know," said Mum. "She's a very thoughtful, beautiful girl too. She's so strong-willed and bold, just like the poppies in the meadow. And she is the princess of all the poppies because she is so imaginative and creative."

"She is a bit of a bossy boots sometimes though," laughed Saffron.

"Ah, but she's my little bossy boots," smiled

Mum. "She's just like I was at her age!"

Saffron smiled and they carried on chatting.

As Poppy made her way back to her bedroom with snacks and drinks, there was no spring in her step and no sparkle in her eyes. Her good feeling had ended. She laid down the tray she was carrying very softly on her toy chest and went to sit on her bed – shifting the sick toys that were in the way.

Honey had made a beautiful job of bandaging a doll's sore head and everything was running smoothly in the Healing Herb Hospital. She looked over at Poppy for approval. Poppy looked away.

"What's wrong, Poppy?" Honey asked, thoughtfully.

She's just so sweet! Ugh! I bet she is never envious of anyone.

"Nothing's wrong, Honey. Why don't you carry on with caring for the dolls and toys?

You are so much better at it than I am!"
retorted Poppy sharply.

Honey knew that this was a nice thing to
say but felt that the way Poppy had said it
definitely wasn't nice. Honey didn't know
what was wrong and she didn't feel welcome
in Poppy's Healing Herb Hospital any more.
She quickly ate her snack, tucked the toys up
in their various beds and told Poppy that she
was going to see what her mum and dad
were doing. Poppy
watched from the
window as Honey
skipped merrily
down towards
the Bakehouse,
her fairy wings
flapping in the
breeze behind
her and her
wand stretched

out in front of her. All the things that Poppy loved about Honey – her calmness, her patience, her kindness and her thoughtfulness – made her feel cross now.

"She's just so perfect!" she exclaimed.

Poppy looked at the chart she had made, with pictures of all the toys. She picked up her pencil and drew a picture of herself with a little heart in her chest and a big arrow pointing to her heart. Then she looked at her healing herb poster but there was nothing there for heartache.

Poppy thought Grandpa might make her feel better so she popped over to see him, but he was busy digging the garden and told her to come back later. Mum was snoozing – all that chatting had tired her out – and Dad was at work, so Poppy decided to go and see Saffron at her shop – maybe they could make up. Poppy decided to take some flowers with her to say sorry about the

mix-up the day before. She picked a lovely
bunch in the garden, tied them up with a
pretty ribbon and attached a note:

Dear Saffron.
I am very sorry
about the mess I
made.
It was a mistake
I PROMISE
love from Poppy
xx

When Poppy arrived at the shop, Saffron
was measuring a customer for a ball dress.

"I'll be free in a minute, Poppy. Just have a
look around the shop," said Saffron. "Or go
downstairs and wait for me."

Saffron's basement was like a lovely cosy
bedroom, with a dressing table which had
perfume bottles on it and beads around an
oval mirror. There was a lavender velvet

armchair with lots of little cushions. Some
were embroidered and some were covered
in sequins. Propped against one of the soft
raspberry-coloured walls was an antique
mirror surrounded by a fancy gold frame.
In the middle of the floor was a patterned
Indian rug woven from rich spice colours.
And there were masses of scarves and hats,
bracelets and shawls lying around, which
anyone could use to dress up the outfit
they were trying on. There was even a
chest full to the brim with bridal things –
lace veils, headdresses, old wedding dresses
and beautiful silk flowers. It was a room fit
for a princess! As Poppy explored the
dressing room, trying on beads and scarves
and prancing around in front of the mirror,
she could hear Saffron talking to her
customer in the main shop.

"You will look wonderful. You really
will be the belle of the ball! I always think

that a new outfit can make you feel like
a different person," trilled Saffron.

Poppy thought about what Saffron had
said and wondered whether she was right.
Could different clothes really make you feel
like a new person? Poppy decided to test
Saffron's theory by trying on some of the
fabulous clothes that were all around her.
She put on a small black hat and a
patterned shawl which she wrapped tightly
round her shoulders.

"I'm an old granny
now!" smiled Poppy.
Next she tried on
a flowery smock
dress and tied
a long scarf
around her
forehead. "Wow!
Now I'm a hippy,"
she laughed.

Then she took a frilly white wedding dress and a veil with a silk flower headdress and dressed up as a bride. *This is fun*, thought Poppy. *I can become whatever and whoever I want, as long as I wear the right clothes – maybe Saffron is right!*

She changed back into her own clothes and all her unhappy feelings came flooding back – what was she going to do?

I would like to be a different person. If I was just like Honey, everyone would like me so much more. I bet if I looked like Honey, it would be easier to act like her too! Then I would be perfect as well, Poppy thought as she looked at herself in the mirror.

She suddenly decided that she didn't have time to wait until Saffron was free – she had better things to do. She laid the flowers and note on Saffron's desk, said goodbye and dashed off before Saffron had a chance to say anything. Poppy had had another one of her good ideas and she wanted to put it into effect – she needed to get home right away.

Chapter Five

Poppy had made a decision. She was going to try as hard as she could to look and act like Honey.

In order to look like Honey, Poppy knew that she would need to raid Mum's make-up bag, wear different clothes and curl her hair. But before she went upstairs to start her physical transformation, Poppy decided that she would practise *being* a little bit more like Honey. She was desperate for other people to think she was as kind and thoughtful as they seemed to think her best friend was.

"Hello, Mum. Did you have a good sleep?" asked Poppy as she walked into the kitchen.

"Lovely, thanks, darling!" replied Mum. "I feel so much better. What are you up to now?"

"Nothing really," said Poppy. "I wondered whether there is anything that you need me to do. I could help you tidy up, or maybe you'd like me to do something in the babies' room."

"Oh, that's very sweet of you, Poppy. Perhaps you could finish off these baby boxes," said Mum. "We need to put in nappies, cotton wool, wipes, talcum powder and vests. I am trying really hard to get everything organized before the twins come, but there is so much to do – including my accounts for Fancy Hats."

"I'd love to do that," said Poppy, although what she really wanted to do was go upstairs and become just like Honey. But she kept

these thoughts to herself as she sorted out all the baby things that Mum had been buying for months now. By the time she had finished, not only did the baby boxes look perfect, she was actually beginning to enjoy herself!

"That's brilliant, Poppy," said Mum. "Well done!"

Then Mum grabbed a stack of baby magazines and went to have a lie down. Another one – Poppy couldn't believe it!

Poppy desperately wanted to surprise Mum with another good deed before she surprised everyone with her new look. She racked her brains, wondering what Honey might do. Then she had another good idea. Honey was always baking cakes and goodies for people, so Poppy decided that she would have a go. But what she forgot was that Honey could do that because her granny ran the Blossom Bakehouse and always helped her! Poppy knew that she wasn't allowed to use the cooker all by herself so she decided to make chocolate crispy cakes, using the chocolate sauce Mum had for ice cream – she was sure that would work just as well as melted chocolate.

Poppy got out everything she would need: cornflakes, paper cake cases, chocolate sauce, a big mixing bowl and a spoon, and then she set to work. She opened the box of cornflakes and tipped it upside down.

Nothing happened at first so she thumped
the bottom of the box and the cornflakes
came rushing out so quickly that quite a few
of them ended up on the floor.

"Never mind!" said Poppy to herself. "I'll
clear up when I've finished."

Next she squeezed the chocolate sauce
onto the flakes, but there wasn't quite
enough so she decided to add some milk.
Granny Bumble was always pouring milk

into mixing bowls – it would probably make the cakes even better than usual! But the milk did not have the desired effect; it just made the cornflakes go soggy. Poppy thought that the mixture would be fine once it was in the little cases. To her dismay, it wasn't. The mixture was so runny that, as she spooned it into the cases, it just ran over the tops and all over the work surface. She decided that she must get the cakes into the fridge as quickly as possible – that would fix everything. But just as she was spooning the mixture into the last case, Mum came into the kitchen.

"Poppy! What on earth are you doing now?" said Mum. "Did I say you could make cakes?"

Poppy shook her head. There was a terrible mess everywhere and horrible soggy cakes. There was no point in saying to Mum that she was trying to be thoughtful.

Mum would never understand – she just assumed Poppy was being naughty.

"Help me with this mess, Poppy, and then go and play in your room," said Mum wearily.

Poppy sighed and did as she was told.

Nothing goes right for me, she thought.

When everything was cleared up, Poppy went to her room. She felt like banging her door *very* hard to show Mum how she was feeling, but Honey would never do such a thing, would she? Poppy gently closed the door behind her. It was a big strain being calm and gentle all the time. Trying to be like Honey hadn't gone very well. Poppy was finding it really hard trying to act differently all the time. Maybe she would do better at just trying to *look* like Honey.

Chapter Six

Poppy mixed some glossy brown poster paint in a tub.

"That will be lovely for my hair," she said to herself.

Then she ran into Mum's room to fetch the curling tongs and make-up. Poppy was feeling better already. In her dressing-up box she found some perfect fairy clothes, just the sort of things that Honey would wear. Poppy didn't want to be a princess any more – she wanted to be a fairy like Honey.

Poppy brushed the brown paint onto her
fine blonde hair. Then she rubbed some of
Mum's bronzer onto her cheeks, nose, chin
and forehead. When the brown paint was
dry, she began to curl her hair with Mum's
tongs. Poppy knew that she wasn't allowed
to plug them in, but she did anyway – how
was she supposed to make ringlets in her
hair with unheated tongs? Mum would
never know.

She knew that Mum would be very cross
if she could see what Poppy was doing. But
what did it matter? Mum always seemed to
be cross with her at the moment – or that
was what it felt like to Poppy.

When she had finished curling her hair,
she turned the tongs off and put them away.
Then she put Mum's make-up back where
she had found it. Poppy slipped into the
clothes she had chosen from her dressing-up
box and then she looked at herself in the

mirror. She was pleased with what she saw –
mainly because she didn't look like herself
any more. Poppy sprinkled herself with fairy
dust to complete the transformation and to
make her feel as calm and gentle as Honey
always seemed to be. Then she decided to go
and show Grandpa her "new look". He
would think she was lovely – just like Honey.

Poppy sneaked out of the house – she
didn't want Mum to see her – and made her

way as quickly as possible to Forget-Me-Not
Cottage, where Grandpa lived. She could see
Grandpa right at the bottom of his garden,
digging the vegetable patch, but as she made
her way towards him, a huge drop of rain
fell on her cheek. She looked up towards the
sky and a heavy shower plunged onto her
face. Poppy let out a small wail – it was
going to ruin her make-up and hair.

Grandpa looked up from what he was
doing and was rather surprised by what
he saw.

"Oh Poppy, it's you!" he said. "I thought you were Honey from a distance. You, umm, look very, umm, nice, but what's the new look in aid of?"

"I just felt like a bit of a change," replied Poppy breezily. "I have to go now, Grandpa, otherwise the rain is going to wash me back to normal! If you would like me to do any jobs for you when the sun comes back out, I would be very happy to help!" she called as she dashed up the garden. "I could wash dirty potatoes – anything!"

Grandpa shook his head. "What a girl!" he smiled to himself. "Wash dirty potatoes indeed! Princess Poppy doesn't usually like to get her hands dirty. What on earth has come over her? It's as if she has changed into a different person!"

Grandpa went indoors and put on his coat. It was time for him to do his shift at the General Store. Everyone in the village was taking turns to look after it while Aunt Marigold recovered from the dreadful flu virus. The village could not cope without supplies.

Poppy looked at herself in the mirror when she got back to her room. She was soaked through. Her hair was streaked with the brown paint and her cheeks were smeared with the bronzer. Some of the paint was even running onto her "Honey" outfit.

I'm going to need something that lasts longer

than this, Poppy thought, and set her mind to coming up with a new plan.

Just then, Mum called Poppy down for their reading time together.

"I'll be there soon, Mum," called Poppy as she dived into the bathroom to wash her face and hair and to change her clothes.

"Have you washed your hair *again*?" asked Mum when Poppy came downstairs.

"No, I just got soaked in the rain when I went round to see Grandpa earlier," said Poppy.

"You poor darling," said Mum and kissed Poppy on the forehead. Then the two of them settled down on the sofa to read together.

"Thank you very much for reading with me, Mum," said Poppy appreciatively when they had finished *Milly-Molly-Mandy* – her favourite book.

"I love reading with you," said Mum as she stroked her daughter's beautiful blonde hair.

"I thought I might pop into the General Store in a hour or so to see how Grandpa is getting on," she went on. "Everyone in the village is doing shifts in the shop until Aunt Marigold is well enough to come back to work. Do you want to come, Poppy, or would you rather stay at home with Dad? He's got quite a bit of work to do so you'd have to be very good for him."

"I think I might stay here with Dad and make some more fairy dust, then tomorrow I could take fairy dust to our friends in the village who aren't feeling well," suggested Poppy sweetly, suddenly remembering about

Aunt Marigold, Mimosa and Madame
Angelwing having flu and still trying her
best to be good.

"What a lovely idea! See, you can be a
good princess when you try," said Mum
proudly. "But what is fairy dust?"

"I made it to cure my sick toys in the
Healing Herb Hospital. It's ground lavender
– it smells very nice and it made all my toys
feel better really quickly," explained Poppy.

"I see," said Mum. "I'm sure Marigold, Madame Angelwing and Mimosa would all love to have some of your fairy dust. I'm very glad that you're behaving so nicely now after the trouble you caused at Saffron's shop and in the kitchen earlier. What a change in you. Well done, darling!"

Poppy smiled. *Maybe* she would have another go at being as sweet as Honey.

Everyone does prefer a good girl, thought Poppy. *I will become the sweetest girl in the village! I know I can do it!*

Poppy spent the afternoon making a poster about her hospital and grinding up some more fairy  dust, but all the time she was worried. She was convinced that Mum and Saffron would like her better if she were more like Honey, and that Grandpa would too. What was it he

had said? "I thought you were Honey . . .
You . . . look very . . . nice . . ." Suddenly it all
seemed so clear to Poppy. When she acted
like Honey, everyone praised her; when she
acted like Poppy, she always got into trouble.
Poppy became even more determined to be
like Honey in every way. Honey was the
photographer's favourite. She was Saffron's
favourite. She was also Miss Mallow's
favourite. Maybe even Mum and Grandpa
liked her best too. Everyone preferred Honey
– or that's how it seemed to Poppy.

Poppy cared about the inside and outside
of herself equally. She knew she shouldn't
mind if other people thought Honey was
prettier than her on the outside, but she did.
And she knew she shouldn't mind if Honey
was gentler and calmer than her on the
inside, but she did. Poppy didn't like any part
of herself any more, and this made her feel
very miserable indeed. And the more

miserable she became, the more her imagination gave her crazy thoughts.

That night Poppy went to bed feeling very sorry for herself and with lots of ideas buzzing around her head as to how she could become more like Honey.

Chapter Seven

"When I was at the bakery earlier, Granny Bumble told me that Honey is going on a trip to a museum today with her parents," said Mum at breakfast. "What would you like to do today, Poppy?"

"Well, you know how I told you I wanted to take my fairy dust to Aunt Marigold, Mimosa and Madame Angelwing? I need more lavender so I thought I would buy some from Sally Meadowsweet at the Garden Centre," said Poppy. "I *will* have to spend a bit of my pocket money but I don't mind at all." And she genuinely didn't mind. In her obsession with imitating Honey, Poppy seemed to have forgotten that caring about other people really *did* come naturally to her; she simply approached things in a different way to her best friend.

Poppy picked up her sparkly purse from the kitchen table and slipped it into her bag.

"That is such a lovely thing to do," smiled Mum. "You are so good at thinking up wonderful ideas and entertaining yourself. I do understand that you are missing Honey at the moment and that I'm not much fun, but you seem to be equally happy in your own company. I'm proud of you."

"Thanks, Mum," said Poppy as she turned to leave.

"Send them all my love," called Mum, "but do make sure you don't outstay your welcome. Sometimes when people are ill,

they get tired very quickly and don't want
visitors to stay too long."

*She's happy with me now — just until the next
time I mess things up*, thought Poppy.

As she got closer to Lavender
Valley Garden Centre, she
could smell lavender in
the air. She loved this
part of the village.
Everything smelled
so gorgeous and it
was very peaceful.
Poppy thought it
was the perfect
place to come

whenever she felt a bit sad — as she did just
now. It was a good place to think. Poppy
was feeling very confused. Every time she
tried to be more like Honey, everything went
wrong and people thought she was being
naughty or nasty. That never seemed to

happen to Honey: Poppy was convinced it was because Honey was naturally nice and didn't need to try.

Poppy was frustrated by her situation and because of this she was growing a story in her own head which wasn't true. She felt as if no one understood her; nothing she did was right. What she didn't realize was that everyone in Honeypot Hill liked her just the way she was – they liked her no more and no less than they liked Honey. The girls were simply different – a good team. But because Poppy hadn't explained how she was feeling to anyone, not even Mum, she had blown everything out of all proportion and she was feeling very sorry for herself indeed.

"Hello, Poppy!" said Dr Latimer. "What's up with you? You look very down in the dumps."

Poppy had been so lost in her own world that she hadn't noticed Dr Latimer walking

along in the opposite direction. Dr Latimer
had known Poppy all her life. Mum said that
he had also brought *her* into the world, so he
had known Mum all her life too. He was a
bit like an extra grandfather so Poppy didn't
feel shy about talking to him at all. She was
so grateful to him for actually asking her
what was wrong rather than being cross
with her that she told him everything. Poppy
explained that she was very sad about
Honey being so lucky and Mum being so

tired and everyone thinking she was naughty all the time, and that she didn't feel like a princess any more.

"Ah yes. Friends and family – so much joy and so much pain. It can be difficult sometimes. I'll have a talk with your mother, Poppy, dear," he promised her.

"Thank you, Dr Latimer," said Poppy, and gave him a hug.

"Oh, and Poppy – one more thing," said Dr Latimer before he started on his way again. "Always remember that you are a little princess!"

Poppy smiled. If *only* she could believe that.

Soon Poppy was at the Lavender Valley Garden Centre. There were several greenhouses as well as fields of flowers and water fountains at the back.

"Morning, Poppy!" called Sally from the big greenhouse.

"Hello, Sally!" replied Poppy as she went

in. "I wonder if I could buy some lavender to take to Aunt Marigold, Mimosa and Madame Angelwing. I use it to make healing fairy dust to make them feel better," she explained.

"Of course you can. I'll help you gather it. Why don't you give them each a posy of flowers as well? You could sprinkle the fairy dust over the flowers. Come on, let's go and see what we can find," Sally suggested. "But I've got an appointment at the Beehive Beauty Salon later this morning so I'm afraid I can't be too long. I'm having my blonde highlights done!"

"What do you mean — blonde highlights?" asked Poppy.

Sally laughed. "Oh, Poppy! That's something you don't have to worry about. I like to brighten up my dull brown hair with blonde highlights, that's all," she explained.

"If they can make brown hair blonde, can they make blonde hair brown?" asked Poppy curiously.

"Lily Ann Peach can do anything you ask her!" replied Sally.

Poppy and Sally stood side by side in the greenhouse and made delightful little posies together. They tied ribbon around the stems of sweet peas, daisies, larkspur and bluebells. Poppy put all the bouquets in a basket and paid Sally for the lavender. But her mind wasn't  on Mimosa, Aunt Marigold, Madame Angelwing and the healing fairy dust any more. All Poppy could concentrate on was what Sally had said about Lily Ann Peach at the Beehive Beauty Salon. Poppy realized the Beehive Beauty Salon was probably where Aunt Marigold had her hair turned bright orange. And now that she knew about Sally's highlights, she wondered whether they could give her hair just like Honey's.

"I must dash now, Poppy!" said Sally as she headed off to the salon. "Send my love to Marigold, Mimosa and Madame Angelwing – I am sure the flowers and your fairy dust will make them well in no time."

Poppy was planning to stay at the Garden Centre and make a bit more fairy dust and then to go around the village with her basket of flowers. When she had finished grinding fairy dust, she sprinkled some onto the posies and headed towards Aunt Marigold's flat above the General Store, swinging her basket of fresh flowers in her hand. But just as Poppy reached the store, Honey passed by in her parents' car.

"Hi, Poppy! Guess what happened to me

today?" said Honey breathlessly as the
car slowed right down. "You know the
photographer who did the photos at
Saffron's shop? He asked me to go up to
the city to do some photos for a big shiny
magazine! I've had the best time and I've
been allowed to keep most of the clothes I
modelled! You can borrow them whenever
you like though," she added.

"Wow! That's amazing! You're so lucky,"
said Poppy as she forced a smile and tried
to feel happy for her friend.

I thought they were going to a museum! I bet Mum lied to me in case I got mad again about missing out on the photographs!

Poppy felt worse than ever. She was definitely not in the mood to hand out flowers with fairy dust any more. Poppy had other plans. She was going to pay a visit to the Beehive Beauty Salon.

Chapter Eight

Poppy had never been to the Beehive Beauty Salon before. She knew that Granny Bumble went there a lot and Mum did sometimes, although not so much since she'd been expecting the twins. Poppy really wanted to see what it was like, but as she opened the door to the salon, she felt quite nervous. A delicious waft of shampoo, conditioner and make-up hit her as soon as she walked in. Poppy thought everything about the salon was wonderful and her nerves melted away.

"Hello, Princess Poppy," said Lily Ann
Peach. "What can we do for you today?"

Lily Ann always looked very glamorous in
Poppy's opinion, with perfect shiny dark hair
and very full pink lips. And she always wore
high heels and had perfectly manicured nails.

Poppy looked around in amazement. There were lots of ladies she knew from the village. Some were having their hair cut. Some were having their nails done. Others were sipping coffee. All were chattering merrily, laughing and telling each other stories about their lives.

"Well, what I was wondering, Lily Ann, is – could you give me brown hair instead of blonde, please? With curls? And brown skin instead of pink?"

"But, Poppy, you have wonderful hair and skin. Why would you want to change them? They suit you so perfectly," commented Lily Ann.

All the other ladies hushed so that they could hear what Poppy was saying. Suddenly the salon was completely quiet.

"Ladies!" said Lily Ann. "Hands up who would like hair just like Poppy Cotton's?"

To Poppy's great surprise they all raised their hands.

"Yes, please!" called one.

"Mine is like the straw at Riverside Stables. Look how soft her hair is!" said another lady kindly.

"I would do anything to have hair like that," said another.

"What are you thinking of, Poppy?" asked Lily Ann.

"I just want dark brown hair and browner skin," mumbled Poppy, looking down at her feet.

"If I had hair like yours, I'd be over the moon, Poppy! It's like spun gold," said Sally Meadowsweet, who was sitting under a great big heater and had lots of foil twisted into her hair.

Poppy blushed. This wasn't working out.

"Never mind. You don't understand. I'm sorry," she said and turned to leave.

"Don't go, Poppy!" called Lily Ann. "Maybe we can help you, sweetheart. If that's what you really want."

Poppy went back inside. Lily Ann sat
her down on a big swivel chair in front of
a mirror. She took Poppy's hairclips out
and began to run her fingers through the
long blonde hair. Poppy felt a little bit
better already.

"Tell me what the problem is. Why don't
you like your glorious blonde hair any
more?" asked Lily Ann softly.

Poppy bit her lip. "It's because Mum and
Saffron were talking and they didn't know I
was listening (and grown-ups say the truth

when they think you can't hear them), and"
– at this point Poppy sniffed and swallowed
– "they said that Honey was beautiful and
sweet and kind. And Mum said she had
lovely dark hair and skin. And not only that:
Honey gets chosen to do everything at
school and ballet. Plus she is taken to lots
of fun places by her mum and dad. All I do
now is tidy the new nursery over and over
again. And, even worse,
Honey is a professional
model now!" Poppy
broke off into great big
sobs. She felt very sad
indeed now that she had
admitted all these things at
once, although it was good to get it all out.

Lily Ann and the other ladies looked
sympathetically towards Poppy.

"And did Mum and Saffron say that you
were *not* pretty and kind?" asked Lily Ann.

"Um, well, no," admitted Poppy. "But they didn't say that I was and that's all that matters."

"Poppy, you are a very special girl and you usually seem so confident, whereas Honey is less sure of herself. Everyone knows that you are a marvellous little princess. There is no need to say it over and over again. But we all think it – don't we, ladies?"

There was a huge chorus of comments from all the dear ladies of Honeypot Hill.

"She's lovely!" said one.

"So kind. Always making gifts and treats for others!" said another.

"She has so many good ideas *and* a great imagination!" said a lady whose head was lying backwards in the sink.

"Princess Poppy, you are a very precious girl. Honey is too. You are different from each other but neither of you is better than the other. Together you are a perfect team! And don't forget that poor Honey only sees her mum and dad from time to time. That's why she's getting so many treats just now. You get to see your parents every day," concluded Lily Ann.

Someone passed a fruit sweet over to Poppy. She dried her eyes and smiled. It was fun in the Beehive Beauty Salon.

"But also," Poppy went on, "I get a bit sad because my mum is working really hard at Fancy Hats so that she can take some time off when the babies are born. And having a super-huge tummy makes her feel really tired too – don't tell her I said that though," she added with a cheeky smile.

There was another chorus of sympathy for Poppy.

"Of course, it's been hard for you lately," said Sally Meadowsweet.

"Yes, poor darling!" said a voice from under a hair dryer. "I always told Lavender Cotton it would hard if she had more children – she and Poppy have been so close."

"Just goes to show you can never guess what little ones are thinking or feeling!" agreed another.

"I'll tell you what I'll do, Poppy," said Lily Ann. "I'll spray your hair brown for fun and put it in ringlets – but I'll have to ask your mum if that's all right. I'll call her. I bet it won't look as pretty as your natural colouring though."

Poppy sat quietly as Lily Ann went to phone Mum. She seemed to be gone for ages.

"Your mum says you are allowed and she's just coming over to meet you and see how you look!" explained Lily Ann on her return.

Lily Ann sprayed a dark brown colour onto Poppy's hair. Then she curled it into little ringlets, just like Honey's. Then she took a big soft brush over Poppy's cheeks with brown powder. Poppy smiled. She thought she looked great. By curling her hair, Lily Ann had made it look much shorter, so it was almost exactly like Honey's.

"Now I look good," she said.

Lily Ann smiled. "But, Poppy, you looked even better as yourself, my love," she said softly. "Just as Honey wouldn't suit your blonde hair."

Poppy sat munching on chocolate chip cookies and sipping a hot chocolate that Belinda, the salon junior, made for her until Mum arrived.

"Poppy!" Mum was shocked. "What *has* happened to your cornsilk hair and rosebud skin?" she asked. "And why did you tell Dr Latimer that you're not a princess any more?"

"Well, you said to Saffron yesterday that Honey had wonderful dark hair and skin," began Poppy, "so I thought—"

"And do you know what else Saffron and I were saying? We went on to say that you are as pretty as a summer's day, with your cornflower-blue eyes and cornsilk golden hair and pale rose-pink skin. And then we said that while Honey is gentle and kind, you are strong and generous and know your own mind. You are like the tall bold poppies growing in the meadow – brave and daring and so very beautiful! And that you are the princess of all poppies because you have good ideas and kind thoughts. You didn't hear all that, did you?" said Mum.

"Um, no," admitted Poppy. "I think I must have already gone back to my room because I was feeling really sad about what I *had* heard." She held onto Mum very tightly.

"Oh, Poppy! You must always come and talk to me if you are ever feeling sad or upset," sighed Mum. "I think you deserve a bit of a treat to make you feel better. What would you most like to do?"

"I'd like to go to a proper palace where a real little princess has lived. Then I will know if I am still a true princess after all," said Poppy.

"Well then, we shall take the train up to the city tomorrow and visit a real palace. Dad will be back from work soon. Why don't you see whether he will help you deliver these lovely flowers? Are you going to come with the brown hair and skin or go back to your own self?" asked Mum.

Poppy looked in the mirror. All the ladies in the salon looked at her.

"I think I'll have it washed off now if that's OK?" she said.

"Hurrah!" all the ladies chorused.

Poppy suddenly realized that people *did* like her as herself. They weren't just saying it to make her feel better.

"Poppy, don't ever keep your worries to yourself. We are all here to help you understand things," said Lily Ann.

Mum nodded in agreement. "No more secrets?"

Poppy smiled. "No more secrets."

As they walked home together, Mum suggested that Poppy change into one of her wonderful princess dresses before she delivered the posies. Poppy thought it was a great idea – it would make her feel like a princess again. Or at least she hoped it would.

Chapter Nine

Back at Honeysuckle Cottage Poppy tried
on lots of different princessy outfits and
accessories, twirling in front of the mirror
each time she put on a different dress.

"I suppose I do still suit my princess
clothes," she said to Ruby. Then she went
to get the basket of flowers and scattered
a little bit more fairy dust over them. She
closed her eyes and chanted a rhyme
which she had just thought of:

Lavender flower, make my friends sing,
Kindest of herbs, good feelings bring!

Then she
decided to
sprinkle a little
fairy dust on
herself too! As
she did so, she
chanted another
new rhyme:

Poppy Cotton, a princess so real,
Let this dust make your heart heal!

Now she was ready for anything.

That evening Dad and Poppy went to visit
Aunt Marigold, Mimosa and Madame
Angelwing to try to make them feel better.
On the way to Aunt Marigold's flat they
bumped into Honey. As usual, she was

dressed in her gorgeous fairy clothes and was carrying her new wand with her – waving it about as she walked.

"Hi, Poppy! Hi, Mr Cotton! Where are you going with those lovely flowers?" asked Honey.

Poppy explained to her what they were doing and then asked her friend whether she would like to join them. Honey jumped at the chance – and she was sure her fairy wand would help everyone get better even faster!

When they arrived at Aunt Marigold's, they found her propped up by pillows in her big bed underneath a lovely patchwork quilt. She smiled and sat up as soon as she saw Poppy, Honey and Mr Cotton.

"What beautiful flowers!" she exclaimed, smelling the posy. "You are sweet."

"I've sprinkled them with my special healing fairy dust too," announced Poppy. "It will make you better really soon! And I've made up a healing chant for you."

As Poppy sang her chant, Honey waved her fairy wand over Aunt Marigold.

Nasty flu-bug, go away,
Listen well to what I say:
I am a princess through and through,
Much stronger than the likes of you!

Aunt Marigold laughed – she was looking better already. Then Poppy told her all about her experiences at the Beehive Beauty Salon – she was sure Aunt Marigold would enjoy hearing all about it.

Poppy was nervous of visiting Madame Angelwing because the ballet teacher was

usually so strict. She had a beautiful cottage
filled with ornate French furniture and
exotic fabrics. When they arrived, they
found Madame sitting up in bed like a
queen. In fact there was no need for Poppy
to be nervous. Madame Angelwing's face lit
up when she saw her two little pupils and
Mr Cotton.

"Darlings! What a pretty picture. All dressed up and flowers as well. Ah! You have cheered me so much. I love pretty things. You see, when I was in the *corps de ballet* in Covent Garden . . ." and Madame launched into one of her exciting ballet stories. The girls were entranced by the tales of ballerinas and tutus and satin ballet shoes – so entranced that they almost forgot Madame's healing fairy chant! Once again, Honey flitter-fluttered her fairy wand over the patient, and Poppy said her rhyme. By the time they had finished, Madame Angelwing looked almost completely well again. She thanked the girls as they left and

said she hoped to be well enough to teach
their ballet classes again soon.

Finally the girls went to see Mimosa.
Sometimes Mimosa came between Poppy
and Honey, but she was friends with both of
them and right now all that mattered was
that she got well again so they could all play
together. When Poppy, Honey and Mr
Cotton arrived, they found Mimosa and her
mum reading together. Poppy and Honey
handed Mimosa her posy and then sang her
a special healing chant:

Fairy girl, so sweet and light,
Please get well again tonight,
Our fairy dust has mighty power,
Coming from a special flower.

Mimosa looked better already! She
laughed and threw her legs out of bed. Her
friends took her hands and they danced a

fairy dance in a circle around the room. As they said goodbye, Mimosa's mum thanked the girls for cheering Mimosa up and said that she was sure Mimosa would be well enough to play with them in a day or so.

Poppy was very glad that she had visited all their friends and given them her gifts, but she was also very tired. She was desperate to go to bed because she was impatient for tomorrow to come. Poppy wanted to see what a real palace looked like and to discover how a true princess lived.

Chapter Ten

Poppy woke up early the next morning and jumped out of bed – she was so excited to be going to a real palace.

She spent ages picking an outfit – it was vital that she looked just right. By the time she came downstairs Mum was beginning to worry that they might miss their train to the city.

"Morning, Mum. I'm ready," said Poppy. "Will you tell me all about where we're going now?"

"First you must have some breakfast and then we really have to go. I'll tell you all about where we're going when we're on the train," promised Mum.

Poppy wolfed down her breakfast, kissed Dad goodbye and then she and Mum left for the Honeypot Hill Railway Station. They caught the train with only seconds to spare.

As soon as they were settled into their seats on the train, Mum told Poppy that they were going to Kensington Palace in London. She explained to Poppy that this was where

Princess Victoria spent her childhood before she became Queen at the age of eighteen.

"Does that mean I'll be a queen when I grow up too?" interrupted Poppy.

"Oh, Poppy!" laughed Mum. "You are funny. You will always be my princess but I'm afraid you will never be Queen because you are not a royal princess."

"I was only joking, Mum! I wouldn't like to be a queen at eighteen years old," said Poppy. "I can't wait to see her princess room though. I imagine she had a fluffy princess bed with wonderful toys around it. And I bet there's a golden ballroom and huge wardrobes filled with pretty ball dresses. I'm sure she would have had an amazing life as a real royal princess. I bet she never wanted to be anyone else."

"Oh, my darling! I'm so sorry that I didn't even notice that you were feeling sad and left out. I just thought you were being

terribly grown up and self-sufficient and
that you didn't like hanging around with
your mum and her big baby tummy any
more."

"But, Mum, I do understand. Really I do.
I just miss you," Poppy confessed.

"And I've missed you too, sweetheart," said
Mum as she gave Poppy a huge hug and
flicked a tear away from her eye. "I still have
time for my lovely princess. I will always
have time for you. Maybe I just need a bit
more help from other people. I've been so
busy making hats, cooking and cleaning.
I know Saffron would love to help but she
has her shop to look after. We'll think of
something."

"Maybe sometimes you and me could
run Saffron's shop and Saffron could come
to our house to look after the twins when
they are born," suggested Poppy.

"We'll see," said Mum. "I'll mention it to

Saffron when we get back from the city."

Just then their train pulled into the station.

They were in London at last. Poppy and
Mum gathered up their things and then
flagged down a shiny black cab. Mum asked
the driver to take them to Kensington
Palace. Poppy felt like a real princess in a
wonderful carriage. By the time the cab
dropped them off at the gates of the palace,
she was almost bursting with excitement.

As they walked up a long path towards the palace, Mum told Poppy the story of Queen Victoria's childhood.

"Her Uncle William was the King and he had no children of his own to take the throne, so when he died everyone realized that this dainty little princess would be the next Queen. She was kept apart from other children and her only friend was her governess, Lehzen."

"What is a governess?" asked Poppy.

"She's a teacher who comes to your home so you don't have to go out to school," said Mum.

"Gosh. I do like Miss Mallow but it would be a bit boring if she was my only friend. I love playing with Honey and Mimosa and the other children at school. And with Daisy and Edward too," Poppy said. "Princess Victoria must have been really sad and lonely. I didn't think I would ever feel sorry

for a real princess. I thought I would feel really jealous!"

Mum laughed.

When they got into the palace, Poppy was quietly disappointed. It was very dark and not nearly as pretty as she had imagined it would be. Mum read the information boards as they explored the palace and told Poppy all about Princess Victoria.

"Poppy, it says here that the palace was freezing cold and filled with creepy-crawlies when the princess lived here nearly two hundred years ago."

"Oooh, that sounds really horrible," commented Poppy, screwing up her face. "Poor Princess Victoria! I'm glad I didn't live in the olden days."

Apparently the little princess had been very lonely in the palace and had longed for fun and friendship.

Wow, I am really lucky after all, thought Poppy. *I've got lots of friends and we have so much fun together.*

"Please can we look at Princess Victoria's bedroom and toys now?" she asked.

Mum took Poppy to the first floor of the palace, where Princess Victoria's bedroom was. This was where she had been when she was told that she had become Queen, Mum explained. Poppy looked around the room – she couldn't believe that it was once the bedroom of a royal princess.

"My room is *much* better!" she cried in surprise as she looked at the lumpy, hard-looking bed and the drab, dull colours on the walls. She imagined a cold winter's day with no heating and long months stretching ahead with no friends coming to play or to

have lunch or tea. She shuddered. Some
other visitors laughed.

"Here are some of Princess Victoria's toys,"
noticed Mum, pointing out a glass cabinet
full of really boring-looking toys.

Poppy looked at a heavy little black dolls'
pram and some plain wooden dolls and
thought privately that she liked her own
toys much more.

"It says here that she loved to dress these wooden dolls as characters from stories she had read. The dolls were like her friends!" said Mum.

"I do that!" exclaimed Poppy. "My dolls are my friends too — but I suppose I have real friends as well!"

In some ways Poppy felt very different from the princess in the painting Mum showed her. But when she imagined Princess Victoria playing with her beloved little spaniel dog, Dash, and dressing up her dolls, Poppy was sure that she would have got along very well with her; she wished she could have known her and helped take away the loneliness she could feel in the palace walls.

"Shall we go and have a look at the gardens now, Poppy?" asked Mum. "We could have our picnic lunch there and then maybe have an ice cream."

"Yes, please," Poppy replied. "It's really gloomy in here."

They sat together on a bench in the beautiful palace gardens and ate the delicious picnic they had brought with them.

"I wonder what Princess Victoria's favourite food was," said Poppy as she nibbled one of Granny Bumble's delicious muffins. "I bet she never had goodies as tasty as this!"

Mum smiled – it had been a really lovely day.

Chapter Eleven

"Well," said Mum as they approached
Honeypot Hill Railway Station. "Now do
you believe that you are a true princess, as
we have always told you?"

Poppy thought for a few moments. "Yes, I
really do believe I'm a true princess," she said
simply. "Because it isn't being royal and
living in a palace that makes you special, is
it? It isn't even really how you look, is it,
Mum?"

Mum shook her head. "It's being kind,

loving and a good friend that makes you
shine like a princess," she said. "Everyone
around you loves you and believes you are a
true princess so you must believe it too."

"I do now, Mum. I really do," said Poppy
as she skipped off the train. "Yippee! Dad's
waiting for us!" she cried.

Poppy jumped into her father's open arms.
"Hi, Dad!"

"Hello, Princess Poppy. You'll have to tell
me all about your day, but first I've got some

good news for you. Aunt Marigold, Mimosa and Madame Angelwing have all got out of bed today for the first time in a week. They're saying your visit has made them well again!"

Poppy smiled proudly.

"Now, come on home. I've got a surprise for you there," said Dad.

Mum looked confused. She didn't know what Dad was talking about. Poppy was so desperate to find out what the surprise was that she ran ahead all the way home. She burst through the front door and there, waiting for her in the sitting room, was a photographer with his camera and lots of fancy lenses. He had set up strong lights and a white backcloth.

"Ah! My model is here at last. What a beautiful girl. These photos are going to be fantastic – perfect for my exhibition," said the photographer.

"Wow!" laughed Poppy as she ran out to tell Mum about Dad's wonderful surprise.

Poor Mum was holding onto Dad as she walked slowly up the hill – it was hard work with her big baby bump! She smiled at Dad and kissed him when she heard what he had arranged.

"See, I do have some good ideas!" said Dad. "And I thought we could put all the photos in a special album as a memento of the day."

"That would be brilliant. Thanks, Dad! I'm just going to see if Honey wants to come too," Poppy explained as she dashed over to Honeypot Cottage to pick up her best friend.

In a matter of minutes Poppy and Honey were in Poppy's sitting room, chatting away to the photographer. Then Dad came in carrying a huge bag.

"Saffron thought you might like to borrow

some clothes from her shop for the photos,"
said Dad as he poured out what seemed like
a mountain of beautiful dresses, skirts, tops,
trousers, scarves and accessories onto the
sofa. Poppy and Honey couldn't believe
their eyes! It was amazing. They each
grabbed a handful of clothes and ran
upstairs to change into them.

Poppy came back wearing a fabulous princess dress with a hot-pink feather boa, some gorgeous beads and a sparkly tiara, carrying her hamster Posy, who was wearing a pink tutu that co-ordinated perfectly with Poppy's outfit! Honey was looking equally wonderful in mint-green chiffon with matching accessories.

Dad looked proudly at Princess Poppy. As far as he was concerned, Poppy was the most adorable princess in the whole world.

After Poppy and Honey had posed like models, pop stars, princesses and fairies for the photographs, Dad took them for a walk to the Lavender Garden.

"Dad, this is my most favourite place in the whole world," said Poppy. "It's much more beautiful than a royal palace."

"I agree," said Dad. "And do you see how every single flower looks different? Every petal is a different size, shape and colour.

But notice how all the flowers are as pretty as each other when they grow side by side!"

Poppy looked at Honey. Honey did look very different to her. And to think that she had thought that looking like Honey and being like her would be the best feeling in the world. But she was happier looking like and being herself. Poppy knew just what Dad meant about the flowers being different but equal.

"Yes, Dad. Honey and I are both equally special, even though we are completely different," said Poppy. "Me and Honey are the perfect team."

Dad nodded and Honey smiled. Thank goodness Princess Poppy was back to being a true princess again.

THE END

Turn over to read an extract from
the next Princess Poppy book,
Pocket Money Princess . . .

Chapter One

Poppy was standing with Grandpa at the ticket office of the train station in Honeypot Hill.

"One adult and one child for Camomile Cove, please," Grandpa said to the ticket inspector just as the train pulled up. They climbed on and set off for the seaside.

Poppy was really excited to be going to Camomile Cove to visit her cousin Daisy – she hadn't seen her for absolutely ages. Grandpa was looking forward to it too because Daisy was always so busy with her friends and her part-time jobs these days that he hardly ever got to see his granddaughter either – not that she was terribly interested in seeing her old grandpa any more!

When they arrived at Shellbay House, where Daisy and her family lived, Poppy could hardly wait to hear all her cousin's news. Poppy thought Daisy's life was amazingly interesting compared to her own.

"Hi, Poppy," called Daisy. "Come on down to the summer house."

"Don't I get a kiss?" said Grandpa to his newly teenage granddaughter.

"Gramps! I don't do kisses any more," laughed Daisy as she led Poppy down the big garden towards the sea.

At the end of the long leafy garden was Daisy's summer house, nestling among tall summer flowers. The little wooden house was slightly raised from the ground and had steps

up to the front door; from inside there was a beautiful view out to sea and along the sandy beach.

"This is so cool. It's like having your own private house, Daisy. You are so lucky!" exclaimed Poppy.

"Yeah, I know. Isn't it fab? Me and my friends Lily and Rose spent the whole of last summer working in here to make it like this.

It was filthy before and full of junk. We cleaned it out and painted and decorated it ourselves – the inside and the outside. It was really hard work, but definitely worth it – it's such a great place to hang out."

Poppy gazed admiringly at her surroundings. Daisy had so many cool things in the summer house. She'd won masses of competitions on her pony, Parsley, and had pinned all her colourful rosettes on one wall in neat rows. There was a stereo, stacks of CDs and a microphone, posters of pop stars, lots of coloured folders, roller blades, handbags, jewellery and pretty little trinkets. Then Poppy noticed that there were loads of instruments: a drum kit, a keyboard, two guitars and a pile of tambourines, triangles, maracas and other shakers.

"Wow! Can you play *all* these instruments, Daisy?" asked Poppy.

"Well, we've just started a band. I play the

116

drums; my best friend Lily plays guitar; my other best friend, Rose, plays the keyboard and we all sing. We don't have anyone doing backing vocals yet," explained Daisy, "but we will soon."

"What's your band called?" asked Poppy,

desperate to hear more about it.

"The Beach Babes," replied Daisy. "We started it last summer and we're getting better and better all the time. We've got about four original songs and we're always working on new ones. At the moment we're practising for the end-of-term competition in two weeks' time. We're going to play one of our new songs. Some of the boys at school are in a rock band called Caves 'n' Rocks and they'll be playing too. Everyone at school has to vote for the band they think is the best! We *have* to win the vote and beat the boys!"

"Do you think you'll be famous?" asked Poppy. "That would be amazing!"